TEX & SUGAR

A Big City Kitty Ditty

by BARBARA
JOHANSEN
NEWMAN

Sterling Publishing Co., Inc.
New York

ACKNOWLEDGMENTS

While I painted the illustrations for this book I listened to a lot of old-time cowboy music. My favorite albums were those featuring Roy Rogers and the Sons of the Pioneers. Their wonderful harmonizing and yodeling, and their songs of the prairies and open skies, put me in a great frame of mind for illustrating the story of Tex and Sugar. "Tumbling Tumbleweeds," written by band member Bob Nolan, will forever be playing inside my head.

I am also grateful to my wonderful editor Meredith Mundy Wasinger. This is our fifth book together.

Last, but not least, hundreds of cows, pigs, chickens, cats, and dogs don't get painted without a great deal of support on the home front. Love and thanks to my best friend and husband, Phil, for giving me the freedom to lose myself in my art.

Library of Congress Cataloging-in-Publication Data

Newman, Barbara Johansen.
Tex & Sugar : a big city kitty ditty / Barbara Johansen Newman.
p. cm.
Summary: Tex Mex Rex and Sugar Lee Snughead, two big city
kitties, find the road to stardom very rocky until they join forces.
ISBN-13: 978-1-4027-3887-6
ISBN-10: 1-4027-3887-0
[1. Singing—Fiction. 2. Cats—Fiction. 3. Stories in rhyme.]
I. Title. II. Title: Tex and Sugar.
PZ8.3.N46452Te 2007
[E]—dc22
2006009405

2 4 6 8 10 9 7 5 3 1

Published by Sterling Publishing Co., Inc.
387 Park Avenue South, New York, NY 10016
Text and illustrations copyright©2007 by Barbara Johansen Newman
Designed by Randall Heath
Distributed in Canada by Sterling Publishing
c/o Canadian Manda Group, 165 Dufferin Street,
Toronto, Ontario, Canada M6K 3H6
Distributed in the United Kingdom by GMC Distribution Services,
Castle Place, 166 High Street, Lewes, East Sussex, England BN7 1XU
Distributed in Australia by Capricorn Link (Australia) Pty. Ltd.
P.O. Box 704, Windsor, NSW 2756, Australia

Printed in China

Sterling ISBN-13: 978-1-4027-3887-6
ISBN-10: 1-4027-3887-0

For information about custom editions, special sales, premium and
corporate purchases, please contact Sterling Special Sales
Department at 800-805-5489 or specialsales@sterlingpub.com.

For every cool kitty or hot doggie
who has followed a dream . . .
    and for the city that beckons.
        —B.J.N.

Tex Mex Rex

wore a ten-gallon hat,
ate beans from a can,
was a real cowboy cat.

But . . .

. . . his songs could put smiles on fields full of cattle and make an old rattlesnake give up her rattle.

Lookin' for fame, Tex moved to the city.

Sugar Lee Snughead could round up the hens

while tamin' the ponies and swillin' the pens. But . . .

. . . her voice called as sweetly as catbirds in June.
She'd quiet whole herds with the hum of a tune.

Tex begged all the networks to give him a spot.

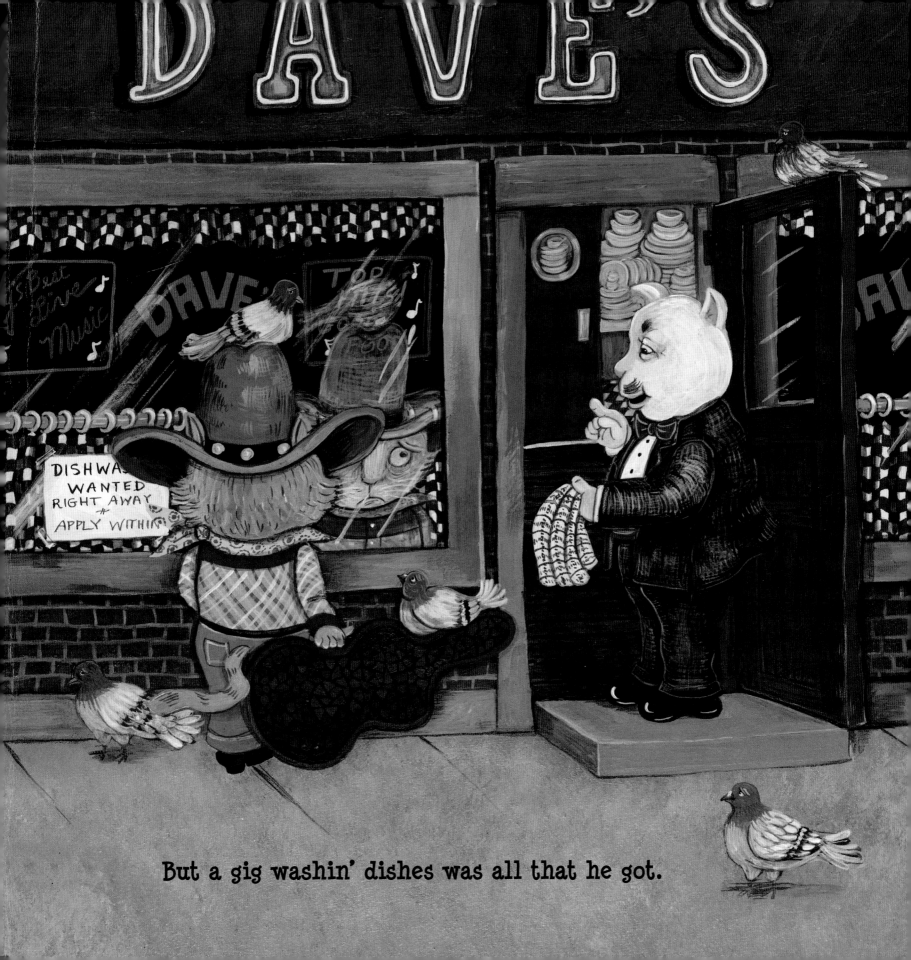

But a gig washin' dishes was all that he got.

She sang
and she danced,
and she flashed her
best smile,

but Sugar's big part in a show was the aisle.

All alone and washed up, sick of bubbles and soap,
Tex figured he'd come to the end of his rope.

One night at work's end, with plates piled high,
he made up his mind to sing songs to the sky.

That very same night, right after the show,
poor Sugar escaped to the subway below.

The "A" train she caught tapped clickety-clacks.
Steel wheels softly wailed as they rocked on the tracks.

The subway's sad song made Sugar decide
to go home and sing at the end of her ride.

Both kitties crooned softly of old country places.
It made them forget about tight city spaces.

The warm summer breeze blew their songs through the sky.
Such sweet, soulful longin' caused neighbors to cry.

The tunes were forlorn
and the feelings so true

that the rats

and the roaches

and pigeons
cried, too.

"Dear Doggies," purred Sugar.
"I hear my soul mate."

"Hot Froggies!" yowled Tex.
"This has to be fate!"

By magic the cats
sang a song they BOTH knew:

"Believe in dreams, darlin'—
You know they'll find you."

At the top of the city
the country cats met.

There were stars in their eyes

as they sang their duet.

With each passin' ballad the kitties soon found
that the sum of their parts was a whole better sound.
The cats became famous! They sang on TV!
Their names brightly blazed on a

BROADWAY MARQUEE.

The music was magic for Sugar and Tex.
It's not hard to figure out
what happened next. . . .

Each cat searched for stardom and found a best friend.
They're still makin' music, and will to . . .

THE END

Daddy~Sitting

For Wilf, Polly, and Bea

Clarion Books
3 Park Avenue
New York, New York 10016

Copyright © 2017 by Eve Coy
First published in the United Kingdom in 2017 as *Looking After William* by Andersen Press.
Published in the United States in 2019.

Clarion Books is an imprint of Houghton Mifflin Harcourt Publishing Company.

hmhco.com

The illustrations in this book were done in watercolor and colored pencil.
The text was set in Mrs Eaves.

Library of Congress Cataloging-in-Publication Data
Names: Coy, Eve, author, illustrator.
Title: Daddy-sitting / Eve Coy.
Description: Boston ; New York : Clarion Books, Houghton Mifflin Harcourt,
2019. | "First published in the United Kingdom in 2017 by Andersen Press."
| Summary: A young girl enjoys taking care of her father through a day of
ordinary activities, and encouraging him to be anything he wants when he
grows up--as long as she can be part of it.
Identifiers: LCCN 2018007703 | ISBN 9781328489890
Subjects: | CYAC: Fathers and daughters--Fiction. | Babysitters--Fiction.
Classification: LCC PZ7.1.C693 Dad 2019 | DDC [E]--dc23
LC record available at https://lccn.loc.gov/2018007703

Manufactured in China
TOPPAN 10 9 8 7 6 5 4 3 2 1

4500693780

Daddy~Sitting

Eve Coy

CLARION BOOKS

Houghton Mifflin Harcourt

Boston   New York

This is Daddy.

Today I'm Daddy-sitting.

He likes to get up early . . .

. . . and dance and sing.

I get him ready.

Then I make his
favorite breakfast.

Daddy is full of energy
and needs lots of exercise.

Daddy-sitting keeps me busy . . .

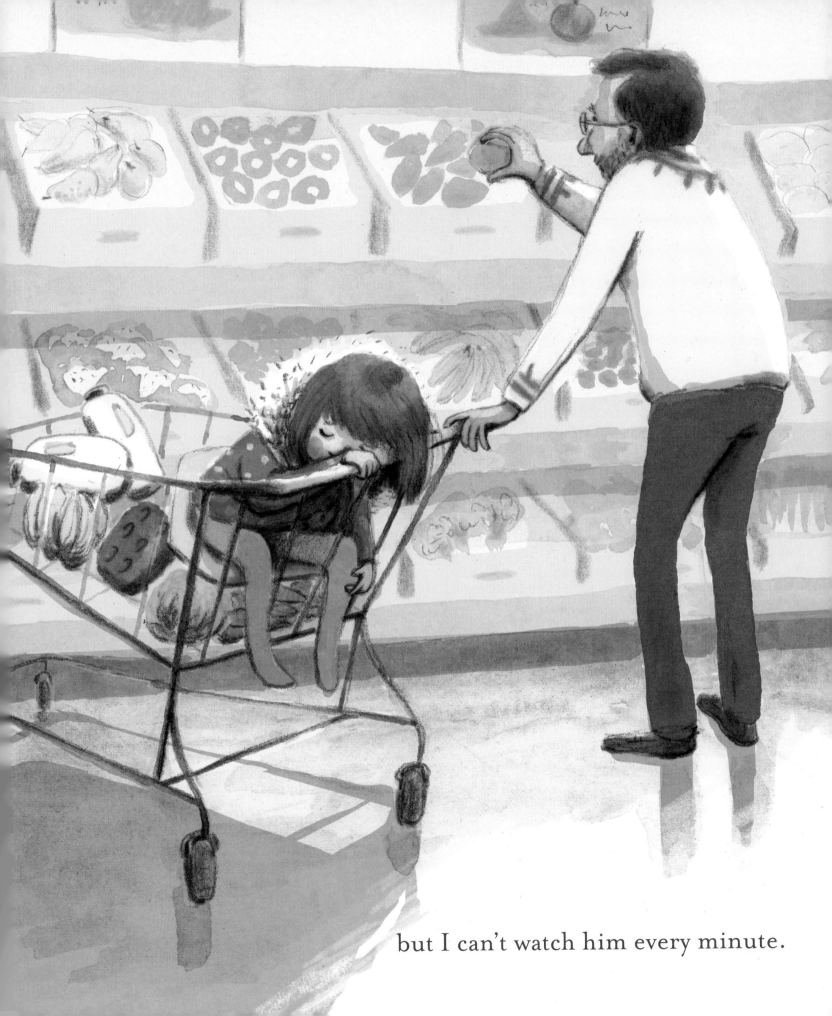

but I can't watch him every minute.

I have lots of jobs to do.

Sometimes he
doesn't watch
where he's going.

Sometimes he just needs a little rest.

Sometimes

he just needs

a little love.

Daddy is very smart.
I tell him he can do anything
when he grows up.

He could be
a lion tamer

or an astronaut.

He could be a famous chocolate maker,

or a detective on the case
of the missing
chocolates . . .

. . . or a nurse treating children
who have eaten too much chocolate.

But Daddy doesn't want
to be any of those.

He wants to do only one job,
which is always packed
with adventure . . .

. . . being my daddy.

And maybe an astronaut,
but only if we can all be astronauts together.